Oscar Goes Indoor Rock Climbing

Story by Pamela Rushby
Illustrations by Amanda Erb

Contents

Chapter 1	Indoor Rock Climbing	**2**
Chapter 2	Just Three Friends	**6**
Chapter 3	Everyone on the List!	**12**

Chapter 1

Indoor Rock Climbing

Oscar's big sister, Georgia, was very excited.
"I'm going indoor rock climbing today!" she said.

"What is indoor rock climbing?" asked Oscar.

"It's a sport that is done inside a big building," said Georgia.
"There are some high climbing walls.
On the walls, there are places to put your hands and feet.
You climb up and try to reach the top."

"Won't you be scared?" asked Oscar.

"I don't know," said Georgia.
"I'll tell you all about it when I get home."

As soon as Georgia arrived home,
Oscar asked her about indoor rock climbing.

"It was so much fun!" Georgia said.
"I climbed to the top of the wall!"

She showed Oscar some photos on her phone.

"I'd like to do that!" said Oscar.
"But the wall looks very high."

"There are some smaller walls for younger children," said Georgia.
"And people even have birthday parties there!"

"Really?" said Oscar. "That sounds like fun."

Chapter 2

Just Three Friends

Oscar's birthday was in two weeks.
He had an idea.

"Mum, Dad," he said. "Could I please have an indoor rock-climbing party for my birthday?"

"Let's find out more about it," said Mum.

Dad looked at the rock-climbing web page on his laptop. "It costs quite a lot of money to go rock climbing," he said. "So, I think you could ask just three friends."

INDOOR
ROCK CLIMBING

Oscar found a pen and paper.
He wrote down the names of his friends from school.
Then he wrote down the names of some friends
from his basketball team.
And some more friends from his guitar class.

He looked at all the names.
Oscar had lots of friends.
"How can I pick just three?" he whispered to himself.

Georgia came into the kitchen.
She saw that Oscar was upset.
"What is the matter, Oscar?" she asked.

"I want to have a rock-climbing party for my birthday," said Oscar.
"But I can't decide who to ask and who to leave out."

"Well, why don't I take you rock climbing
for your birthday?" said Georgia.
"But I would only have enough money to take *you*."

Oscar thought about what Georgia had said.
He wanted to go rock climbing,
but he wanted to have a party with his friends, too.

Maybe there was a way that he could do both.

Chapter 3

Everyone on the List!

Oscar asked Mum, "If I had a birthday party here at home, how many friends could I have?"

"Well, a party at home won't cost as much as indoor rock climbing," Mum said. "So, I think you could ask ten friends."

Oscar looked down at his list. There were more than ten names.

"What about twelve?" he asked.

"How many names are on your list?" asked Dad.

"Only seventeen," said Oscar, smiling.

Mum and Dad laughed.

"*Only* seventeen?" said Mum. "You might as well ask them all, then!"

On Oscar's birthday, all seventeen friends from his list came to his house.
They played games and ate party food.
They all said Oscar's party was great.

The next day, Georgia took Oscar indoor rock climbing.

The wall looked quite high.
But by the end of the day, Oscar had climbed right to the top.

And he was not scared at all.